Max Is Shy

Dominique de Saint Mars

After finishing her degree in sociology in 1981,
Dominique de Saint Mars started writing
children's stories. She writes stories
about children that explain their emotions.
She smiles when she says that she has
interviewed at least 100,000 children.
Her two sons, Arthur and Henry,
were the first to inspire her !
She has won several awards for her cartoons
on parent-child relationships. She is the author of
We're Going to Have a Baby, *I'm Growing Up*,
and *Boys and Girls*.

Serge Bloch
Illustrator

Cathy Mini
Colorist

Original Edition © Calligram, 1992
All rights reserved for all countries
Edition The Child's World, 1993
Printed in the USA

ISBN 0-89565-977-8

De Saint Mars, Dominique.
Max Is Shy/written by Dominique de Saint Mars.
p. cm.
Summary: Max's sister helps him overcome his shyness
and meet a new neighbor.
ISBN 0-89565-977-8
[1. Bashfulness – Fiction.   2. Brothers and sisters – Fiction.]
I. Title.
PZ7.D4488.5May 1992
[E] – dc20

92-17996
CIP
AC

About me

Max Is Shy

Dominique de Saint Mars

Serge Bloch

The Child's World

OK, so I'll go... I'll just say to them: hello!... no, hi!... my name is Max... maybe, instead... have you seen Pompom?... that's my cat!

Wasn't that the kid who lives next door?
Is he coming over?
He didn't say anything. He's probably too stuck-up.

Is this your cat? She came over to my house. I live down at the end of the block.
Oh, Pompom!

I'd like to play with them.
They look like they're having fun.
HI Hi Hi
HA HA HA

Are you ?

Are you always shy
or just once in awhile ?

Are you afraid of what others will think of you
or that they will laugh at you ?

Do you think you're not as good
as other people ?

Are you more shy
around adults or kids ?

Are you more shy
with boys or girls ?

Do you think you are the only person
who is shy ?

Do you try to make friends by asking people questions,
by helping them out, or just by smiling at them ?

Do you bring your games over to play
with people ?

To feel good about yourself, have you ever made a list
of everything you know how to do ?

Do you feel comfortable with who you are,
even if you're too tall or too short ?

Are you able to say, "Sure, I'm shy!"
instead of trying to pretend you're not?

Have you ever met someone
who was more shy than you, and really nice ?

**After thinking about
these questions about shyness,
why not talk them over
with your parents and your friends !**